Millie-Mae

Loves to
Play

Millie-Mae

Loves to
Play

Natalie Marshall

Kane Miller
A DIVISION OF EDC PUBLISHING

Millie-Mae
Dresses Up

One morning Millie-Mae discovers a pink envelope in her mailbox. It's an invitation to a dress-up party.

Millie-Mae
explores the dress-up
box in her bedroom. Which
costume should she wear to the
party? Millie-Mae can't decide,
so she tries on some of her
dress-up costumes.

How about a ladybug,
or an explorer with binoculars?

She could be a tiger with a great big roar,
or a robot with special powers.

At the bottom of her
dress-up box, Millie-Mae
discovers her favorite
costume of all.

Millie-Mae loves her fairy princess
costume with its glittery pink wings
and pink crown. She is all ready
for the party.

Have a fun time, Millie-Mae!

Millie-Mae
in the
Garden

Millie-Mae wakes to the warm sun
shining down on her house. It is
a lovely day to play in her garden.

Millie-Mae
can't go out in her
pajamas. She needs to dress
in her outside clothes.
Millie-Mae chooses her
favorite blue dress.

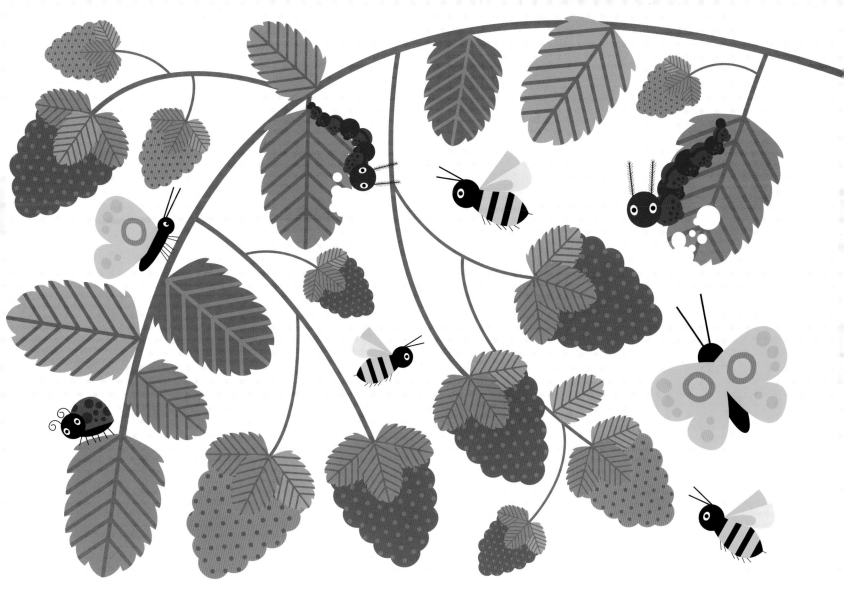

Millie-Mae searches for the little creatures that live among the raspberries. They are having a busy time.

Millie-Mae
waters her plants.
They need a drink every
day – just like she does!

She picks oranges from her favorite tree. Millie-Mae loves her garden!

Millie-Mae
and the
Windy
Day

Millie-Mae wakes up to the sound of the wind blowing through the trees outside her house.

It is a very windy day.

Millie-Mae
wonders what to
do on this windy day.

Then Millie-Mae remembers
that her kite is in the red box
under her bed – perfect!

Millie-Mae must put the kite together before she can fly it.
She ties on the tail of the kite and a long piece of string
to hold on to. Millie-Mae's kite is ready to fly!

Millie-Mae puts
on her hat and coat.

She takes the kite outside in
her wagon. It is still very windy
and Millie-Mae can feel the
wind on her face.

Millie-Mae holds tight to the string as the wind catches the kite and it flies up into the sky, high above the trees.

Millie-Mae loves windy days!

Millie-Mae
and the
Lemon
Tree

Millie-Mae has spent the morning picking lovely
fresh lemons to make something special.

Millie-Mae is going
to make lemonade!

She collects what she needs
from the kitchen, including a
pitcher of water, sugar, and three cups.

Millie-Mae is ready to make lemonade.
First she squeezes the lemons. Then she mixes
the lemon juice with water and a little sugar.

The fresh
lemonade is ready.

Remember to pour
three cups, Millie-Mae!

Millie-Mae and her friends
sit under the lemon tree to
enjoy their lemonade.

Delicious!

First American Edition 2021
Kane Miller, A Division of EDC Publishing

Illustration and text copyright © 2020 Natalie Marshall

First published in 2020 in Australia by Little Hare Books,
an imprint of Hardie Grant Egmont.

For information contact:
Kane Miller, A Division of EDC Publishing
P.O. Box 470663,
Tulsa, OK 74147-0663
www.kanemiller.com
www.usbornebooksandmore.com
www.edcpub.com

Library of Congress Control Number: 2020936872

Printed in Shenzhen, Guangdong Province, China
ISBN: 978-1-68464-212-0
1 2 3 4 5 6 7 8 9 10